YO GABBA GABBA!

BABY TEETH FALL OUT, BIG TEETH GROW!

ADAPTED BY MAGGIE TESTA
BASED ON THE SCREENPLAY "TEETH"
WRITTEN BY SCOTT SCHULTZ

ILLUSTRATED BY MIKE GILES

Simon Spotlight
New York   London   Toronto   Sydney

Based on the TV series Yo Gabba Gabba!™ as seen on Nick Jr.™

SIMON SPOTLIGHT An imprint of Simon & Schuster Children's Publishing Division 1230 Avenue of the Americas, New York, New York 10020
Yo Gabba Gabba! TM & © 2010 GabbaCaDabra LLC. All rights reserved, including the right of reproduction in whole or in part in any form.
SIMON SPOTLIGHT and colophon are registered trademarks of Simon & Schuster, Inc.
For information about special discounts for bulk purchases, please contact Simon & Schuster Special Sales
at 1-866-506-1949 or business@simonandschuster.com.
Manufactured in the United States of America 0710 LAK First Edition 10 9 8 7 6 5 4 3 2 1 ISBN 978-1-4424-0627-8

It was snack time in Gabba Land, and Muno was about to sink his teeth into a juicy, green apple. *Crunch!* Muno took a big bite.

"Whoa!" Muno cried. Something felt strange in his mouth.

"What's wrong, Muno?" asked Toodee, running over to her friend.
"I was eating an apple, and my teeth started to wiggle," replied Muno, looking scared.

"That's okay, Muno," said Toodee. "That means your baby teeth are coming loose."

"Baby teeth? But I'm not a baby," said Muno.

"I know," said Toodee. "They're just called baby teeth because they're the first teeth you get when you're a baby. When you grow bigger, your baby teeth fall out."

"Fall out!" said Muno. "But I like my teeth!"
"Don't worry, Muno," said Toodee.
"Everyone's baby teeth wiggle and fall out.
Now it's your turn."

Muno's baby teeth wiggled some more and soon . . . *Plop! Plop!* Muno's two front teeth fell out of his mouth and into his hand!

Muno and Toodee ran over to tell Foofa what had happened.
"Guess what? Both of my teeth fell out!" Muno told Foofa.

"Wow, Muno, that's great!" said Foofa.
"Yeah!" said Muno. "They just wiggled right out!"

"I guess that means the Tooth Fairy is coming!" said Foofa.

"The Tooth Fairy?" asked Muno. "Who is that?"

"The Tooth Fairy is a special friend," Foofa explained. "If you put your baby tooth under your pillow while you sleep, the Tooth Fairy will visit and take your old baby tooth. She'll give you a surprise in return."

"I love surprises!" exclaimed Muno.

"When my teeth fell out, the Tooth Fairy gave me two gold coins—one for each of my teeth," Toodee told Muno. "I used them to buy my really cool ice skates. I love the Tooth Fairy."

"Razzle-dazzle!" said Muno. "It's time for me to go to sleep so the Tooth Fairy will come."

That night, while Muno was sleeping, the Tooth Fairy came and visited him. She loved the two teeth he left her, so she gave Muno two gold coins.

When Muno woke up the next morning, the first thing he did was look under his pillow.

"Wow! Two gold coins!" Muno exclaimed. "I love the Tooth Fairy!"

"DJ Lance! DJ Lance!" Muno called. "I have two gold coins."

"Congratulations, Muno," said DJ Lance. "Would you like to buy
something with them?"
"Yes," Muno replied.

DJ Lance walked over and grabbed his tray full of toys.

"Each one of these prizes costs only one gold coin," he told Muno.

"You can choose the pet horse, the diamond ring, or the cowboy hat."

Muno didn't have to think very hard. "I'll take the pet horse and the cowboy hat. I love cowboys!"

Muno ran over to his friends to tell them about the Tooth Fairy. "The Tooth Fairy left me two gold coins, and I bought a cowboy hat and a horse with them."

"That's great, Muno," said Foofa. "I told you the Tooth Fairy is so nice."

"Muno, you look kind of funny without your front teeth," Brobee teased.

"I know," said Muno. "It's hard to speak sometimes too."

"Don't worry, Muno," said Plex. "Your big teeth will grow in really fast."

Just as Plex finished speaking, Toodee noticed something. "Look, Muno. A big tooth is already growing in!"

"Wow!" said Muno. "And I can feel my other tooth growing in too!"

Before long both of Muno's big teeth had grown in all the way. Muno smiled. "My new teeth are supersizzling!"